POINDEXTER
Makes a Friend

MIKE TWOHY

A PAULA WISEMAN BOOK
Simon & Schuster Books for Young Readers
New York   London   Toronto   Sydney

For Linda, Clare, Evan, and Mom

SIMON & SCHUSTER BOOKS FOR YOUNG READERS
An imprint of Simon & Schuster Children's Publishing Division
1230 Avenue of the Americas, New York, New York 10020
Copyright © 2011 by Mike Twohy
SIMON & SCHUSTER BOOKS FOR YOUNG READERS is a trademark of Simon & Schuster, Inc.
For information about special discounts for bulk purchases, please contact
Simon & Schuster Special Sales at 1-866-506-1949 or business@simonandschuster.com.
The Simon & Schuster Speakers Bureau can bring authors to your live event. For more information
or to book an event, contact the Simon & Schuster Speakers Bureau at 1-866-248-3049
or visit our website at www.simonspeakers.com.
Book design by Lizzy Bromley
The text for this book is set in Centaur.
The illustrations for this book are rendered in ink and watercolor.
Manufactured in China
0211 SCP
2 4 6 8 10 9 7 5 3 1
Library of Congress Cataloging-in-Publication Data
Twohy, Mike.
Poindexter makes a friend / Mike Twohy. — 1st ed.
p. cm.
"A Paula Wiseman Book."
Summary: Poindexter is a very shy pig who, while helping out at the library,
meets a turtle who is also shy, and together they read a book about making a friend in four easy steps.
ISBN 978-1-4424-0965-1 (hardcover)
[1. Bashfulness—Fiction. 2. Libraries—Fiction. 3. Friendship—Fiction.
4. Pigs—Fiction. 5. Turtles—Fiction.] I. Title.
PZ7.T9314Poi 2011
[E]—dc22
2010018489

first
edition

Poindexter lived in a white house on Brussels Sprout Lane with his mom and dad and little sister, Rose. He was a very shy pig.

Whenever Poindexter's aunts and uncles came over to visit, Poindexter hid under the carpet. They would say nice things like, "My, you've grown so much since the last time we saw you!"

Lots of kids lived in Poindexter's neighborhood
and he wanted to be friends with them.

Sometimes they would tap on his window and ask if he wanted to come out and play. Poindexter wanted to join them, but for some reason, instead of saying yes, he would look down at his feet and blush and make up some silly excuse.

Then he would do what he enjoyed most.
He would put his stuffed animals in a big
circle around him and read them a story.

Poindexter's favorite place to go was the public library.

That's where he could sit by himself and read.

The librarian, Mrs. Polen, let Poindexter push the book cart between the stacks and even put books back on the shelves.

One day when Poindexter was helping at the front desk, a turtle came into the library. He looked around at the huge room with so many books everywhere. And when a few of the kids who were reading stopped and looked over at him, he quickly pulled his head into his shell.

"May I help you?" asked Mrs. Polen.

After a long wait, a small voice came from inside the shell. "Do you have any books on how to make friends?"

Mrs. Polen said, "Yes, we do," and she turned and asked Poindexter if he would like to help her by showing the turtle the how-to section.

The turtle followed Poindexter, and when they got to the how-to section, Poindexter, after searching for a moment, pulled out a book. He handed it to the turtle.

"I'm not very good at reading big words yet," said the turtle.

"Oh," said Poindexter. "This book is called *How to Make a Friend*. If you want me to read it to you, I will—but you should bring your ears up more."

"Okay." Poindexter cleared his throat and started reading. "'Follow the four steps in this book and you will start making friends. Step one is smile. A smile is a good way to show someone you would like to get to know them better. It also says, "I am not a grump."'"

Poindexter tried on a little smile himself and asked, "Are you ready for the next step?"

"I'm still practicing smiling," said the turtle.

" 'Step two is give your name. Tell your name and ask their name.' My name is Poindexter. What is your name?"

"My name is Shelby. This isn't as hard as I thought. Does the book say when you can stop smiling?"
"No. It doesn't tell you that."

"'Step three is share,'" continued Poindexter. "'Sharing is giving away something to someone else to make them happy. The best kind of sharing is giving something you secretly wish you could keep. Good sharing is not giving up things you do not want, like old food or an ugly shirt.'"

Poindexter was suddenly interrupted. A long, dirty, pink snout pushed in between them.

"Hey, could you guys help me find a book? Moles don't see very well," he said, pointing to his squinty little eyes.

The turtle popped his head partway up.
"Would you like to read my book?" asked
Shelby. "It has a good beginning."

"I guess so," said the mole, who carried *How to Make a Friend* over to a table and sat down.

"Would you like me to find another book for you, Shelby?" asked Poindexter.

He walked a little way down the row and came back with one titled *How to Play with Stuffed Animals*. "I've read this book about a hundred times."

They started looking at the pictures together, when the mole returned with *How to Make a Friend.*

"You can have this book back," said the mole. "I don't like it."

"The problem might be that you have been holding it upside down," Poindexter said, turning it around and handing it back to Shelby.

"The book I really came here for is *How to Read in a Dark Tunnel*," said the mole.

"Here it is," said Poindexter, "and it's printed in large letters." Shelby tried a little smile, but the mole didn't see it.

"I'm glad to get my friend book back," said Shelby. He asked Poindexter, "Would you please read some more?"

"'Step four is be nice. Say something nice to someone to make them feel special. If you notice they have done something well or are wearing something that looks good on them, let them know. Try not to say that you can do it better or that you have a nicer one at home (even if you do).'"

"You sure are a good reader," said Shelby. "You read like a grown-up!"

"Thank you," said Poindexter. "You are a very good listener."

"Could we come back to the library tomorrow and read *How to Make a Friend* again?" asked Shelby.

Poindexter thought for a long moment and said, "I don't think we need to read this book again, Shelby. Why don't we check out the stuffed animals book instead and go to my house and play?"

"Okay," said Shelby, pulling some stuffies out of his shell. "I always keep my favorites with me."

Poindexter and Shelby took *How to Play with Stuffed Animals* to the front desk and Mrs. Polen checked it out.

They walked down the steps of the library, carrying
the book together.